Also by Susan Hughes
Bailey

PUPPY PALS

Riley

SUSAN HUGHES

sourcebooks
jabberwocky

Published by Sourcebooks Jabberwocky, an imprint of Sourcebooks, Inc.
P.O. Box 4410, Naperville, Illinois 60567-4410
(630) 961-3900
Fax: (630) 961-2168
www.sourcebooks.com

Originally published as Riley Knows Best in 2013 in Canada by Scholastic Canada Ltd.

Library of Congress Cataloging-in-Publication Data

Names: Hughes, Susan, 1960- author. | Murch, Jeanine Henderson, illustrator.
Title: Riley / Susan Hughes ; [illustrations by Jeanine Henderson Murch].
Other titles: Riley knows best
Description: Naperville, Illinois : Sourcebooks Jabberwocky, [2016] | Series:
    Puppy pals; 2 | "Originally published as Riley Knows Best in 2013 in
    Canada by Scholastic Canada Ltd." | Summary: Riley helps Kat realize that
    a new female is not mean.
Identifiers: LCCN 2015044675 | (alk. paper)
Subjects: | CYAC: Dogs--Fiction. | Animals--Infancy--Fiction. |
    Friendship--Fiction.
Classification: LCC PZ7.H87396 Ri 2016 | DDC [E]--dc23 LC record available at
https://lccn.loc.gov/2015044675

Source of Production: Versa Press, East Peoria, Illinois, USA
Date of Production: June 2016
Run Number: 5006765

Printed and bound in the United States of America.
VP 10 9 8 7 6 5 4 3 2 1

For a terrific trio:

Marilena Georgiou,

Alexander Logue,

and Zackary Logue

Kat was lying on the grass. Puppies were running everywhere! A tiny pug puppy licked her cheek, while an energetic Jack Russell jumped over her chest. Beside her, a young dalmatian playfully wrestled with a German shepherd.

Kat was surrounded by lovable puppies!

"Kat?" a voice called.

Kat's mother joined her on the lawn. "Pick your favorite puppy, Kat!" she said.

But how could Kat possibly pick just one? They were all so sweet. Look, the tiny shih tzu could

fit in the palm of her hand. The adorable black Labrador was dancing around, begging her to play. The red setter pup was as gangly as a newborn lamb...

"Kat-nip!" the voice called again, louder this time.

Kat sighed and opened her eyes. Her daydream was over. She knew she wasn't really allowed to get a dog.

"Hey, lazybones, I'm here!" Her best friend Maya was standing over her. "Come on. Let's get going!"

Kat jumped up. It was time to head to Tails Up!, the dog-grooming salon owned by Kat's aunt. Aunt Jenn was so busy, she needed help. She had asked Kat and Maya to give her a hand.

"Coming!" Kat said.

The two girls hurried off toward the salon.

"Sorry I couldn't go to Tails Up! right after school today," said Maya. "But there was no way Mom would let me miss my piano lesson. The new puppy will be waiting for us, right?"

"That's what Aunt Jenn said. I wonder what kind of puppy it will be," Kat said.

Her heart felt fluttery. Would it be a low-to-the-ground dachshund? A shaggy sheepdog pup? A ready-for-anything border collie?

"Your aunt didn't tell you?" Maya asked.

"No," said Kat. "When she called this morning, we only talked for a minute. It was kind of an emergency. She asked if we were free to look after another puppy this week. When I said yes, she hung up quickly. She had to call the customer and let her know it could come to board at Tails Up!"

Maya grinned. "I'm so excited, I'm bouncing!" she said.

And she was!

Maya looked at Kat. "Let's run, okay?"

"Great idea!" agreed Kat.

Kat and Maya took off down the sidewalk. When they came to the main street, they turned the corner and sprinted past several stores and a restaurant.

Panting, the girls came to a stop at Aunt Jenn's salon: Tails Up! Boarding and Grooming. The bell jingled as they pushed open the door and went inside.

There was no one at the front desk to greet them. Kat's aunt hadn't hired an assistant yet.

She had just opened her business a few weeks ago. She didn't think she'd be so busy. But every day the waiting room was full of people bringing in their dogs for grooming. That's why Aunt Jenn needed Kat and Maya to help out.

Today was just as busy. A young girl was standing next to a West Highland white terrier. A balding man was holding a Chihuahua in his lap. Another man was sitting alone, waiting while his dog was groomed. He was snoring gently, his chin on his chest. A big man, he had a pushed-in nose, a jowly neck, and a wrinkly face.

"English bulldog," Maya said with a quiet giggle. It was one of their favorite games. When she and Kat saw a new person, they named the dog breed that best matched him or her.

Kat nodded. Perfect.

Just then, Aunt Jenn burst out of the grooming studio. She was wearing her pink grooming apron. Her brown hair was pulled back into a ponytail. "Churchill is all set to go," she chirped. At the end of the leash was a dog with a pushed-in nose, a jowly neck, and a wrinkly face.

"An English bulldog! Nice one, Maya," whispered Kat, squeezing her friend's arm.

"Of course, his short coat didn't need to be clipped. But I gave him a good brush," Aunt Jenn explained to the man. "And I gave his face a good wash, especially in his wrinkles on his nose. That needs to be done once a week. I also clipped his nails."

"Thank you," said Churchill's owner gruffly, his cheeks wobbling as he paid.

"Kitty-Kat, Maya!" said Aunt Jenn after he'd left. "Are you ready to meet our newest guest?"

The girls looked at each other. It was time! They couldn't wait to meet the new puppy!

CHAPTER 2

The girls followed Aunt Jenn into the doggy day care room. Four large dog kennels lined one wall of the room. And there in the last one stood a beautiful golden retriever puppy. As soon as she saw the girls, she wagged her tail and perked up her ears.

"Say hello to Riley," said Aunt Jenn. "She's a three-month-old golden retriever."

The girls dropped to their knees beside the kennel. The puppy pushed her nose against the bars. Kat poked her fingers through, and the puppy licked them eagerly.

"Oh, she's so sweet," said Kat.

"She's amazing," breathed Maya.

"Riley's family, the Baxters, brought her home about four weeks ago," said Aunt Jenn. "But the mom and dad didn't know their daughter has a severe allergy to dogs. Ever since Riley came to their home, the little girl has been sneezing and wheezing. She even has hives on her face and chest."

"Oh no," said Kat. "That sounds horrible." It made her itchy just thinking about it.

"She's allergic to the dog's dander, which is little flakes of its skin," Aunt Jenn explained. Then she winked. "My doggy data for today."

Kat smiled. She hoped that one day she

would know as much about dogs as her aunt did.

"So what are they going to do? What's going to happen to Riley?" asked Kat. She gazed at the plump little pup.

"Well," said Aunt Jenn, "the Baxters know they can't keep her. So they are trying to find her a new home. They think they may have found one, but the new family needs a few more days to decide. Getting a new puppy is a big responsibility."

The girls looked at each other. They knew it, all right. That's why their own parents wouldn't let them get dogs. They said they didn't have enough time to look after puppies.

"The Baxters called me early this morning. They asked if Riley could stay here for a few days until they work everything out. I told them I was busy, but I would check with my helpers." Aunt Jenn smiled at Kat and Maya. "They were thrilled when I called them back and said Riley could come."

"You're the best, Aunt Jenn," said Kat. She knew her aunt had a soft spot for every dog she met. She could never say no to a puppy in need.

"Now, girls, Riley needs lots of exercise. The holes in the backyard fence have been fixed—only a dog Houdini would be able to get out of there! So you can give Riley a good run-around outside. Oh, and the Baxters were beginning to teach Riley some simple commands. Please practice those with her. There is 'sit,' and this is the hand command." Aunt Jenn dropped her arm and opened her hand, palm out. Then she slowly lifted her hand.

Kat tried it. So did Maya.

"And there's 'lie down,'" Aunt Jenn said, pointing sharply to the ground. "The Baxters were also teaching Riley to come. They call 'come' to her when she's on the leash. That way, they can pull her toward them if she forgets what to do. She gets a treat when she does what they ask."

Aunt Jenn handed them Riley's leash. "So, girls, are you okay with your newest little charge? Do you remember how to take a puppy in and out of a kennel safely?"

"You bet, Aunt Jenn," said Kat happily. "And don't worry. We'll take good care of her."

"Okay. Heigh-ho, heigh-ho, it's back to work I go!" Aunt Jenn sang. She smoothed down her apron, and off she went.

As her aunt left, Kat carefully opened the kennel door, reached in, and scooped up Riley. She stood, pressing the golden retriever pup close to her.

Oh, she felt as soft as she looked! Kat breathed in the lovely puppy smell.

Riley looked up at Kat, her eyes sparkling. Most of her body was a beautiful light-gold color. Her hair was fluffy, like feathers. She had a little black nose and dark-brown eyes.

"Here you go, Maya," Kat said, setting the puppy carefully into her friend's waiting arms.

"Riley! Nice to meet you, girl," said Maya gently. She stroked the puppy's soft, golden fur. "You are such a good girl."

Riley licked Maya's hands. The puppy began to wiggle and squirm. She was so happy to have company. And now she wanted to play!

"Okay, Riley," said Kat. "Let's go outside!"

Kat gathered up some chew toys and dog biscuits and led Maya and Riley out into the sunny backyard. The yard was covered in grass, and there were trees along one side. A chain-link fence went all the way around.

"Here you go, Riley," said Maya, setting her

down. For a moment the puppy just sat, looking and listening, her ears turning this way and that. Then she bounded off across the lawn, her tail high.

Riley sniffed the bottom of one tree, investigating all the way around it. Then she raced off to another tree and did the same thing. Suddenly she barked with her paws stretched out in front and her hind end up. She was excited by something in the dirt.

"What is it, girl?" asked Kat.

The girls raced over to look.

"Ants!" cried Maya, laughing. "Black ants!"

Riley barked and barked, wagging her tail, backing away from the insects.

"You are so brave and fierce," Kat teased the puppy.

"Thank you for protecting us," added Maya.

Riley chased a bird and tumbled into a small flower bed. She scratched an itch on her side with her rear paw and fell over. She found a stick and chewed it. She was so busy!

"Okay, let's play ball!" suggested Kat. She threw a ball across the yard. Riley raced after it and chomped it.

"Now bring it here," called Maya, but Riley wouldn't. She stood watching the girls, wagging her tail. Kat went over to take the ball from her mouth, but Riley thought it was part of the game and raced away. The girls laughed.

"Okay, I have an idea," said Kat. She had another ball with her. She threw it down to the other end of the yard. Riley galloped to it and dropped the ball in her mouth. She picked up the new one. When Kat went and picked up the first ball, Riley didn't mind. She just wagged her tail, waiting for more fun. And when Kat threw it, Riley dropped the second ball and raced to pick up the first one.

"Well, this will work for now!" said Maya. The girls took turns throwing the balls for Riley, over and over again.

Finally, the puppy seemed to tire.

"Time for your lessons," Kat announced. She snapped the leash onto Riley's bright-red collar. She and Maya practiced *sit* and *lie down* with Riley. They rewarded her with dog biscuits when she did what she was asked. They also worked on asking her to *come*. If she didn't head toward them when they called, they pulled gently on the leash, drawing Riley to them. When she was close, they praised her and petted her.

When Aunt Jenn came to the door to call them in, it seemed far too soon. "Did it go all right?" she asked. "Will we see you tomorrow?"

"We'll be here," Kat said happily.

Nothing would keep her and Maya away!

CHAPTER 3

ome on, Kat!" Aidan called. "You're so slow. We'll be late."

Kat hurried to catch up with her brother.

She was old enough to walk by herself now, but they still walked to school together every day. They didn't really talk much. Aidan was always listening to his music. But Kat didn't mind. Somehow it was just a nice way to start her day. The bell rang as Kat and Aidan hurried through the fence that circled Orchard Valley Elementary School.

"Later, alligator!" Aidan said, heading to the eighth-grade entrance.

"Bye, bye, horsefly!" Kat replied. She could see her fourth- and fifth-grade class lining up outside the school. But instead of hurrying there, she ran over to Maya's line.

Kat and Maya were both in fourth grade, but this year Kat was in one split class and Maya was in the other. This was the first year they weren't in the same class. It was hard to get used to.

Still, the girls always tried to say hello before school. And share a joke.

Kat ran up to Maya, who was smiling.

"Joke of the day: What did the tree say to the squirrel?" Kat panted.

Maya thought hard. "That has to be an easy

one." Her class line began moving. "Oh, Kat, you never give me enough time," she complained.

"Take as much time as you need! See you at morning recess," Kat teased.

"No way! You always do this. Tell me the answer now!" Maya demanded. But her line was moving away. "Oh, Kat, you're the worst!" Maya turned with a flounce and followed it in. But she lifted her hand, and she gave Kat a quick backward wave to show she was joking.

Kat hurried to catch the tail end of her own line. Even though school had started only a few weeks ago, Kat had a feeling it was going to be a long year. She liked her teacher, Ms. Mitchell, but she really missed having Maya in her class. She was trying to make the best of it, but it wasn't the same without her.

Today, however, there was a surprise for the class.

Ms. Mitchell was standing at the front with a girl beside her. The girl had red hair in long braids. She was wearing a dress with red flowers on it. Her knees had Band-Aids on them. She

wasn't smiling. Her arms were straight down at her sides.

"Please sit down on the carpet, everyone," Ms. Mitchell said.

The teacher bent down and spoke to the girl. The girl just stared straight ahead.

Everyone had already guessed, but Ms. Mitchell said it anyway. "We have a new girl in our class. Her name is Grace."

The girl looked up. She had beautiful soft-brown eyes. But her face was stony. And she stared at everyone, one by one. Kat wouldn't be surprised if the new girl was scared about starting a new school. But she didn't look scared at all. She looked…mean.

Megan and Cora were sitting next to Kat, whispering and giggling.

"Say hello to Grace, class," Ms. Mitchell said.

"Hello, Grace," said everyone except Megan and Cora.

Kat said it too. And, right then, Grace looked at her.

I hope she doesn't think I want to be her friend. The thought popped into Kat's head, and she quickly looked away.

"We're happy to have you with us, Grace," Ms. Mitchell went on in a friendly voice. "Would you like to tell the class anything about yourself?" She waited, but Grace didn't say anything.

Megan and Cora laughed. Grace frowned.

"Well, maybe later," Ms. Mitchell said with a smile. The teacher began to talk about the plans for the day.

Megan nudged Kat. She had finally stopped giggling. "The new girl. What's her name?" she whispered, pointing at Grace.

Megan never listened. Ever.

"It's Grace," Kat answered, annoyed. And, of course, just at that moment, Grace was staring right at them. Great. Now she would know that Kat was talking about her. What if she thought Kat was making fun of her? Just great.

Kat got a bad feeling in her stomach. And then, before Kat could look away, Grace opened her eyes wide. She lifted one lip and made a face at Kat. A really mean face.

CHAPTER 4

Kat gulped and quickly looked at the floor.

If she were in a new class at a new school, she'd be nervous. She was sure of it. Grace was new, but she didn't look at all nervous. She just looked angry.

"Okay, class," said Ms. Mitchell. "Go to your seats, please. Get out your math workbooks."

Kat went to her desk. Ms. Mitchell followed her. As Kat sat down, the teacher stood next to her.

"Josh," Ms. Mitchell said to Kat's seatmate.

"Would you mind moving to one of the long tables? There's a seat in between William and Angela. I'd like Grace to sit here, next to Kat."

"Sure, Ms. Mitchell," said Josh.

Kat watched unhappily as Josh grabbed his things from inside the desk and hurried away.

"Grace, you'll sit here for now," Ms. Mitchell said.

Grace didn't speak. She just dropped into her seat.

"Here's our math textbook and a workbook," Ms. Mitchell said. She left the books on Grace's desk when she didn't take them.

Kat glanced over at Josh. He was talking happily to William and Angela.

It wasn't fair! Why did Grace have to sit here, beside *her*?

"Grace, I'm sure you and Kat will get along," Ms. Mitchell said. "Kat always seems to have a good joke to share!"

Oh, great. Ms. Mitchell had put Grace here because Kat liked to tell jokes. *That's a good reason to never tell a joke again*, Kat thought to herself.

Ms. Mitchell returned to the front of the classroom. She began to explain how to do the math problems written on the board. Kat tried to pay attention. She liked math. But Grace was distracting. The girl put her pencil on one finger, like a teeter-totter, and she used another finger to rock it back and forth. It clicked on her desk each time it hit.

Kat wanted to ask Grace to stop playing with the pencil. But, more than anything, she didn't want to talk to Grace. Grace made her feel uncomfortable. So Kat decided to try to ignore her.

Finally it was recess. Kat and Maya met at their usual spot, under the oak tree by the school gate.

"Okay. Spill. What did the tree say to the squirrel?" Maya said, hands on her hips.

Kat smiled. "Leaf me alone."

Maya smacked her forehead with her hand. "You call that a joke?" she moaned. Then she grinned. "My brother will love that one. Tonight. Dinner table." Then Maya asked, "So, did you bring the Puppy Collection with you?"

"Right here," Kat said. "Voilá!" She presented it just like a magician. She'd been holding it behind her back, hidden in a black bag.

She and Maya didn't want anyone else to see it. They worried the other kids might laugh at them. Like Megan and Cora. Kat knew for sure that they'd tease her. For some reason, they liked to try to embarrass her. Of course, they had been better lately. Ever since Kat had told them to leave her alone.

Kat and Maya sat down and opened their

scrapbook. Puppies were the best things in the world. But neither girl was allowed to have one. So they did the next best thing: they collected photos of their favorite puppies or drew pictures of them. They gave each puppy a name and wrote a description about it. It was like having their own collection of puppies. Usually they found the pictures online or in magazines, but they'd also decided to add puppies they met.

Maya turned to the latest page, and a black, curly-haired puppy looked up at them. "Don't you wish we could really meet Lollie?" she said. "She looks so cute! Look at her tiny black nose."

Kat read aloud: "*Lollie is a toy poodle. She has so much energy! You can't hold her back for even a minute. She jumps so high, it's as if her back legs are springs. She is very smart too.*"

Maya turned to another page. "Here's sweet little Bailey," she said. She was looking at a photo of a golden-yellow puppy. Bailey had been a guest at Tails Up! a few weeks ago, and the girls had helped take care of him.

"It was so much fun playing with Bailey," said Kat. "Remember how soft his fur was? Remember how he'd shake his chew toy in his mouth?"

Maya smiled. "Here's what we wrote: *Bailey is a Labrador retriever puppy. He is eight weeks old. He is being housebroken, and he is doing well! Bailey likes to chase toys and shake them. He is very gentle. He likes to give us kisses.*"

Then Kat sighed. "Oh, I miss him. But now we have Riley to play with! Won't it be great to see her after school?"

"I can't wait," said Maya. "She's so pretty. Such a beautiful golden color."

"Hey, did you notice that Riley's ears were darker than the rest of her coat?" Kat asked. "I was reading about golden retrievers last night. They can be any color from cream to gold. If you look at the ears of a golden retriever pup, you can tell what color her adult coat will be!"

"Einstein! That is so cool," said Maya. She

looked at Kat admiringly. "You know a lot about different dogs."

"All thanks to the magic of the Internet," Kat said, spreading her hands wide.

The bell rang to end recess, and Kat closed the scrapbook.

"Hey," said Maya. "Our teacher told us that you have a new girl in your class. That's great, right? You're lucky."

Kat lifted her eyebrows. She put the Puppy Collection back into the bag. "Not great. And I can already tell that she isn't very nice."

"Seriously? You can already tell? You just met her."

"Yeah, I can tell," Kat said.

"How?" Maya asked, surprised. "What did she do?"

"Well, nothing really," Kat said. "She just looks mean. And I have to sit beside her." Then she said firmly, "I don't like her."

Suddenly someone moved.

Someone who had been standing on the other side of the oak tree. Someone they hadn't seen there.

Kat turned. That someone was Grace.

Oh no! Kat's face turned red. She felt terrible. Had Grace heard her?

Kat opened her mouth to speak, but Grace turned and walked away. Kat jumped to her feet. She knew she should follow the new girl. She knew she should speak to her and say she was sorry.

But she didn't move.

"Who was that?" Maya asked. Her large

brown eyes were concerned. "What's wrong, Kat?" Then, a moment later, her face cleared. "Oh, that was her, the new girl. Right?"

Kat nodded. "Yeah, it was Grace. Do you think she heard me say I didn't like her? And that she looks mean? She may have seen the Puppy Collection. What if she tells everyone about it, just to get back at me?"

"Well, we'll just have to hope for the best," Maya said with a shrug. "Maybe she didn't hear or see anything. Plus, you only just met Grace. You don't really know what she's like yet."

The teacher on recess duty was ringing her hand bell and walking toward the girls.

"Come on, Kat-Nip, let's go." Maya gave Kat's hair a gentle pull. "Hey, you can apologize to her when you get back to class. You sit beside her, right?"

"Yeah," Kat said. Although she was really confused. She didn't know what she wanted to do. Grace had started it all by making that mean face. Hadn't she?

Maybe she would apologize. Or maybe she wouldn't.

CHAPTER 5

As Kat went into her classroom, she had a funny feeling in her stomach. She knew she couldn't talk to Grace about what had happened. Not yet.

Kat sat down without looking at the new girl.

"Time for our library visit," Ms. Mitchell said. Kat felt better. She'd forgotten that it was library day. Thank goodness! She could avoid Grace for a little while longer.

Kat grabbed her library book from her library bag. Then she rushed to the back of the classroom to line up. When her class went to the library, they had to walk in partners. Grace was still sitting at her desk, and Kat didn't want Ms. Mitchell to force her to be Grace's library partner.

But who would Kat walk with? She had been Heather's buddy last week. But today Heather had already partnered up with Sarah.

Ms. Mitchell was looking at Grace. Then she turned toward the back of the room. Was she looking for Kat? Frantic, Kat turned to the closest person. It was Owen. His best friend, Ari, was away sick today.

Kat stopped to think. Would Megan and Cora tease her if she asked Owen to be her partner? They said he was in love with her, just because he blushed when she talked to him.

Should she do it? Grace still didn't have a partner. Ms. Mitchell was coming toward Kat.

She had no choice. "Owen," she blurted out. "Buddy up?"

Owen blushed. "Okay." He nodded.

Kat stood next to him, uncomfortable. She watched as Ms. Mitchell spoke softly to Megan and Cora. Gently, the teacher encouraged Grace to stand beside the two girls.

Then Ms. Mitchell led the line out of the classroom. Kat didn't want to look, but she couldn't help it. Grace walked along beside Megan and Cora like a gloomy shadow, her face down, her braids dangling.

She'll find a friend eventually, Kat told herself, trying not to feel guilty. *If she can stop looking so scary.*

The class listened as the librarian talked to them about nonfiction books and how to search for them on the shelves. Then they were given ten minutes to think of a subject they were interested in and find books about it.

Picking a subject was easy for Kat. Dogs, of course. And she even knew where to search on the shelves, because she'd done it so many times before. It was especially nice because Megan and Cora were in a completely different aisle of books.

Kat buried her face in her book. She didn't even look to see where Grace was or how she was doing.

But then Owen came over and began looking at books on the shelf right below hers.

"Looking up dogs?" Owen said, without

looking at Kat. "I know how much you love them."

"That's right." Kat glanced over at him. She was curious to see what he had picked. "I didn't know you were interested in…" Kat peered at the cover of the book he was reading. "Pigs."

Quickly Owen slammed the book closed and looked at the cover. He blushed. "Oh," he said. "Pigs? Oh, well, not really."

Kat tried not to grin.

Owen shoved the book back on the shelf and grabbed another one. He seemed to begin reading at a random page.

Kat peeked over Owen's shoulder. "Owen, I didn't know you could read upside down," she said.

Owen's face was totally red. "Oh, right. Um, see you," he said and hurried away.

When it was time to return to class, Kat and Owen walked back together. Kat saw Megan and Cora pointing at them. The girls were whispering to each other. They ignored Grace, who trailed behind them. Her face was like a mask.

Lucky for Kat, the rest of the afternoon went quickly, with no shared seat work. She was able to avoid talking to Grace. In fact, she hardly even had to look at her!

When the bell rang at the end of the day, Kat met up with Maya at their usual spot. They hurried to Tails Up! and checked in with Aunt Jenn.

"Hello, little Riley!" the girls called as they burst into the doggy day care room. They rushed over to Riley's kennel. The golden retriever puppy jumped up. She wagged her tail and wiggled happily.

"Here we go. Out you come!" said Kat. As she held the puppy in her arms, all her troubles melted away. She bent her head to breathe in Riley's sweet smell. She felt a soft, wet nose press against her chin. Riley's tongue gave her a quick kiss.

"Do you want to hold her?" Kat asked Maya.

"No, just put her down so she can run free," suggested Maya. "She's probably excited to be out of her kennel!"

Kat set her down, and Riley raced straight over to Maya to say hello. Then she ran straight to the back door, sat down, and looked back at the girls with her beautiful brown eyes.

Kat and Maya laughed.

"Okay, we understand!" Kat said. "You want out, right?"

The girls grabbed Riley's chew toys and several dog biscuits. When they opened the door, Riley went tumbling out into the backyard. Just like yesterday, she raced across the lawn. She investigated each of the trees, sniffing all the way around. She explored the flower beds. She barked at a squirrel. She grabbed a stick and growled, shaking it in her mouth. The girls laughed again.

"Let's give her some time to burn off

some energy before we do her lessons," Kat suggested.

"Good idea," Maya agreed. "Hey, so did you apologize to the new girl this afternoon? Grace, right?" She looked at Kat curiously. "You didn't say anything about her on the way over here."

Kat sighed. She explained that she had chosen Owen as her walking buddy to the library just to avoid Grace. And that even though Megan and Cora had left her alone, Owen had followed her around.

"Well, you did encourage him," Maya teased. "Poor boy. He just wants to be near you."

Kat raised her eyebrows.

"Sorry, Miss Sensitive." Maya grinned. Then she frowned. "But what about Grace? You didn't say sorry to her?"

Kat shook her head and looked away. "No. Not yet," she said.

Kat pointed at Riley and laughed. "Oh, look, Maya!" she cried. "Riley is trying to sniff the flowers!"

The golden retriever pup was in a small garden. She was fascinated by a plant with beautiful yellow blossoms. The plant was taller than her, and the blossoms towered above her. But she was determined to sniff them. She

raised her head as high as it would go, but she couldn't reach.

"Riley's up on her back paws! She's balancing!" Kat said.

Sure enough, Riley balanced for about five seconds and took one sniff of the blossom. Then she snapped at it and toppled over into the flowers.

"Riley!" cried Maya, concerned.

But Riley bounced back up like a rubber ball. She wagged her tail and came running. Her eyes were sparkling. Her mouth was full of yellow petals.

"Oh, Riley. Naughty girl," Kat told the puppy. She tried to make her voice sound stern, but it was hard. Little Riley looked so proud of herself!

"Okay, Riley. Time to do some more training now," said Maya firmly. "Right, Kat?"

Kat nodded.

"Okay. Riley, sit, girl. Sit." Maya raised her hand, palm open, as Aunt Jenn had shown her.

Riley looked up at Maya and wagged her tail. A petal dropped from her mouth. Kat tried to hide a giggle.

"Sit, Riley," Maya repeated. She lifted her palm again.

Another petal fell.

Kat didn't speak. Neither did Maya. Both just looked at the pup and waited.

Suddenly Riley sat. Just like that.

"Good girl, Riley," Maya said, stroking Riley's soft head. "Well done." She gave the puppy a biscuit.

Kat clapped her hands together. "Nice one, Riley!"

For the rest of the afternoon they reviewed *sit*, *lie down*, and *come* with the pup. Finally Riley lay down and wouldn't get up. She was exhausted.

"That's all for today," Maya told her. "We

have to go now, but we'll be back tomorrow."
Riley wagged her tail happily as Maya picked
her up.

Kat sighed as she followed Maya and Riley
back inside. When puppies were happy, they
wagged their tails. When they were sad or
lonely, they whimpered. When it was time for
a walk, their eyes lit up.

You could always tell when a puppy was
happy or sad or excited. It never tried to hide
its true feelings. It never tried to pretend it was
something it was not. And it was hard to hurt a
puppy's feelings.

But Grace, Grace was different. What was
she actually like? Was she mean or not? Why
was it so hard to tell? *Why aren't people more
like puppies?* Kat wondered.

CHAPTER 6

The next morning, Kat still hadn't decided whether or not to apologize to Grace. Then she was late, so she didn't even have time to say hello before the class started. Not that she was too sorry about that.

Kat waited to see if she and Grace would have to do shared seat work. Instead, Ms. Mitchell began to teach the class about a kind of poetry called Japanese haiku. She told them that a haiku is a short poem with three lines. The first line has five syllables, the second line has seven syllables, and the third line has five syllables.

Ms. Mitchell read the students some examples of haiku. Then she asked them to write their own poem.

Kat looked at Grace out of the corner of her eyes. Grace's chin was tucked down. Her hair fell in front of her face so Kat couldn't see it.

Kat was relieved. She doodled little drawings of puppies across the top of her page as she thought.

A pug puppy. A Nova Scotia duck tolling retriever puppy. A Great Dane puppy.

Then she began to write. It took her a few tries.

Puppies

Wiggly, wobbly, soft
Mouth smiling, eyes so trusting
Puppies are the best

Not bad, Kat thought, nodding her head.
But when she looked up, Grace was staring
right at her page. She was reading Kat's poem!

Grace's own paper was blank.

I bet she's going to copy my haiku, thought Kat angrily. And, sure enough, just then Grace bent over her own notebook and began to write.

Grace was a copycat.

Then Kat smiled. She couldn't help it. *A copycat copying a poem about puppies!* The idea gave her the giggles.

Kat survived until the bell rang for lunchtime. She met up with Maya, and they went to her house to eat.

After lunch, she managed to avoid Grace. But, when Kat came in from afternoon recess, Grace's desk was smack up against hers. Maybe someone had bumped it when they had left for recess. Maybe someone had pushed it too close.

Grace wasn't there yet, so Kat got up and grabbed the edge of her desk. She would just move it back to where it had been. It didn't have to be so close. She gave it a shove.

"Hey!" It was Grace, and she was glaring at Kat. Her arms were straight down at her sides, and her fists were clenched.

Kat's stomach tightened. "I was just..." she began.

"Yeah, I see. I know," Grace said in a tight voice.

Kat could tell she was trying not to yell. Just then Ms. Mitchell called, "Okay, class. Attention, please."

Grace sat down, and Kat did too. She kept her eyes on the front of the classroom where Ms. Mitchell was starting her lesson.

But then something caught her attention. She stole a look.

Grace was pulling a folded note out of her desk. Grace's name was on the outside of the piece of paper. She read the note, and then her face went hard, like stone. The note must have said something nasty.

Grace scrunched the paper up into a little

ball and jammed it back into her desk. She didn't even look at Kat, but Kat felt a sinking feeling. Grace had seen Kat shove her desk. She knew Kat didn't like her. For sure Grace would think Kat had put the note in her desk.

Kat wondered what it had said. How bad it could have been. Part of her wanted to blurt out that she didn't write the note. That she'd never do anything so mean. But the other part of her was too afraid to talk to Grace. She looked so angry. Kat was afraid of what Grace might say back to her.

Finally the bell rang to end the day. Kat had never been so happy to leave her classroom. It felt like she was escaping something.

Maya was waiting by the oak tree. When she

saw Kat's face, she frowned. She put her hands on her hips. In a silly voice, she said, "Listen, girlfriend, I am so over this. You're turning into a total drama queen!"

Kat knew Maya wanted to make her laugh, so she tried to smile. The girls set out for Tails Up!, and Kat told Maya about what had happened with Grace's desk and the note.

"What did the note say?" Maya asked.

"I don't know," Kat replied. "But it really upset Grace. And I mean *really*."

Kat paused, hoping her friend would say something comforting. She didn't.

"Sorry, Kat. But you're probably right," Maya said. "Grace will think it's you who wrote the note."

Kat nodded glumly.

"But, hey, what do you care anyway?" said Maya. "You don't like Grace."

"I don't like her, but it's not nice for someone to hurt her feelings on purpose," said Kat. "She may not like me either, but I don't want her to think I'm mean. I don't want her to think that I'd write a rotten note about her and stick it in her desk!"

"Well, if she knew you at all, she'd know you could never do that," Maya said, as they reached the main street in town. "There isn't a mean bone in your body."

Kat was silent. She wanted to think that was true, but it wasn't. She had plenty of mean bones. For example, when she was little, she had knocked on old Mrs. McCormack's door and then run away. Lots of times, when she'd done something bad, she'd tried to make it look like it was her brother's fault.

"Hey, let's forget about Grace for a while," Maya said, interrupting Kat's thoughts. "Look, we're almost at Tails Up! We have something much better to do than worry about that new girl, right?"

"You're right," said Kat. She would put Grace out of her mind. They were going to play with Riley! What could be better?

CHAPTER 7

A bout half an hour later, Kat and Maya reached the park. They still couldn't quite believe it. They were there with a real live puppy! Riley trotted along at the end of her leash, excited as ever. She saw a leaf blow past and chased it. Then she saw a pine tree, and she stopped to sniff at the trunk.

"Riley is so much fun to watch!" Kat said, grinning. "She's interested in everything!"

The girls kept walking, and so did Riley. But instead of walking with the girls, Riley went around the tree. She suddenly reached the end of her leash and had to stop. Puzzled, she looked at Kat and Maya. The girls grinned back at her.

"Now what, Riley?" Maya challenged her.

The perky puppy tried to run to her, but her leash was wrapped around the tree.

"You have to go back around, Riley," Kat told her. "Like this!" Kat ran around the tree, unwrapping the leash as she went. Riley greeted her with wiggles and a wagging tail.

"Good girl, Riley," said Maya. She stroked the puppy's soft fur. Her ears felt like velvet.

The girls and the puppy walked across the grass. There were several rows of trees and bushes along one side of the park. There was a playground at one end. At the other end was a hill with a grove of trees on top. The hilltop was Kat's favorite place in the park. From up there she could see the town on one side and the countryside on the other.

Kat laughed again. Riley was staring in amazement at a squirrel, sitting on a tree branch, chattering angrily at her. The puppy barked at the squirrel and wagged her tail.

"I don't think he wants to be your friend, Riley," said Maya, smiling.

The girls persuaded the playful pup to leave the squirrel. Then Kat cried, "Okay, let's go! Let's run, Riley!"

The girls raced across the grass, and Riley galloped along with them. When they reached the other side of the park, Riley flopped down, exhausted, her tongue hanging out.

"Are your little legs tired, girl?" Kat asked with a grin.

But only a few minutes later, the golden retriever pup had bounced back up. She was exploring the grass, sniffing here and there.

"Let's run back again," suggested Kat.

"How about you go with Riley. When you turn around, I'll call her. Then you can run back with her," Maya suggested.

Kat poked her in the arm. "You just want to rest!" she said.

Maya did a pretend pout. "Well, really. How insulting." Then she grinned. "Yeah. You're right. So go, okay?"

"Let's run, Riley!" cried Kat. "Come on. Let's go!"

Riley looked up at Kat and smiled. As Kat

began running, the puppy leaped excitedly beside her. Kat had to be careful not to get tangled up in the leash!

They ran all the way to the rows of trees and bushes and then stopped. "Good girl, Riley," Kat said. She reached down and rubbed the pup's head.

But Riley was pulling at the end of the leash. She was looking into the trees and wagging her tail.

"What is it, Riley?" Kat asked. "Do you see something in there?"

Riley was wiggling happily. She continued to pull toward the trees.

"What is it, girl? Another squirrel?" Kat asked, letting herself be led into the bushes. But then she stopped. She saw what Riley had seen.

It was Grace. The girl was sitting there, among the trees. She had a book on her lap, but she wasn't reading. She was staring off into space. And she wasn't smiling.

CHAPTER 8

Kat froze. Her mouth dropped open. She felt the bad feeling again. She wished they had stayed at Tails Up! Coming to the park had definitely *not* been a good idea.

Grace looked up and saw Riley and Kat.

"Oh!" she said, getting to her feet. She wore a blue T-shirt and shorts. Now her face was tilted down. "I was just… I live near here," she went on. "Right beside the park." She started to sound angry. But Kat hadn't even said anything.

Riley wagged her tail even harder. She pulled at her leash, wanting to go to Grace.

"Is this your dog?" said Grace. She pulled on one of her auburn braids.

Kat didn't answer. She was still surprised at finding Grace.

Riley stopped pulling. Now she sat nicely. She looked up at Grace, waiting to be petted.

Grace didn't come any closer.

"Tell me," she said to Kat, "is she yours?" Her eyes were fixed on the puppy. Now her hands were bunched up into two fists.

Kat felt an angry red flush travel up her face. This was the girl who had made a really mean face at her. Who had probably copied her poem about puppies. It was because of her that Kat had to be Owen's hall buddy back and forth from the library. And now here she was, getting in the way of Kat's time with Riley.

Grace took a step closer to the puppy. Suddenly her face was scrunching up. She took another step, moving closer to them.

Kat didn't move. She was scared. Grace looked angry again. Why was she making fists? What if Grace hit her? What if she hurt Riley?

Quickly Kat looked over her shoulder. Where was Maya? What should she do?

Riley whimpered. She jumped up and wiggled with her whole body, trying to get to Grace. Kat couldn't believe it. Why on earth was this sweet little puppy being so friendly to the mean girl?

Then Grace said softly, "I love dogs, especially puppies." It was almost like she was talking to herself. Her eyes were shining. "Can I pet her?"

Kat wondered what to do.

Grace's face got that mean look on it. Then tears began to trickle out of the corners of her eyes. "Can I? Please?" she asked. Her voice sounded funny.

She was crying! Grace was crying!

"Her name is Riley. Pet her," Kat blurted out. "Go ahead."

But Kat was too late. Just as she spoke, Grace ran past her and across the park.

Riley watched the girl go, her head tilted to one side.

Kat watched her go too. She opened her mouth to call to her, but no sound came out. She thought about chasing after her, but couldn't decide if she should.

Suddenly Maya was coming through the bushes toward her.

"Where did you and Riley go?" she called as she came close. "I was waiting for you two to run back to me. Were you hiding from me? Trying to teach me a lesson, right?"

Then Maya looked more closely at Kat. "What is it?" She touched Kat's arm. "Did something happen?"

Kat nodded her head. She was confused by what had happened. "Grace...Grace was here. She was sitting right there, reading. Riley must have heard her in here, so she dragged me in." Kat spoke slowly, explaining. "Grace asked me if Riley was my puppy and whether she could pet her, and I didn't answer. Maya, she seemed so angry at me. I thought she might hit me. Or hurt Riley."

"Oh, boy," Maya said.

She sat down in the leaves. Kat sank down beside her. Riley immediately jumped into Kat's lap for a snuggle.

"I was scared, so I didn't say anything. I couldn't speak or move." Kat rubbed Riley's plump tummy.

"Wow," Maya said softly.

Kat thought for a minute. "But maybe I've been wrong about Grace."

Maya lifted her eyebrows. "What do you mean?"

"Riley was so sweet to Grace. She just wanted to say hello. She wanted Grace to pet her.

Maybe Riley is trying to tell me something. Maybe I haven't really given Grace a chance. Maybe she isn't as mean as I think." Kat's voice was quivering.

"Kat, Riley is just a puppy. Puppies love everyone," Maya said.

"Well, maybe," Kat said. "But still. Riley seemed so happy to see her. It was like she wanted to make Grace feel better. There must be a reason for it." Kat buried her face in Riley's fur. "You know, Grace is new. We should feel sorry for her. And she does seem to like dogs."

Maya stared at her. "Seriously? I can't believe you're saying that, Kat," she said. "You're not saying you want to be her friend?" She paused. "You're not saying you want us to be her friends."

Kat shrugged. "I don't know," she said, and it was true. She was confused by her feelings.

Kat would do anything for a puppy who needed her help. That was easy. So, why was it so much harder to do something for a person, a new girl in her class?

CHAPTER 9

The next morning, Kat still didn't know what to do about Grace. She tried to think about puppies while she waited for her brother. *Puppies here, puppies there. Puppies, puppies, everywhere...*

But it didn't work.

Then she tried to think about Riley. *Sweet little Riley, with her beautiful brown eyes, her silky-soft ears, and her big, floppy paws...*

But that didn't work either.

All Kat could think about was Grace.

I've got to speak to her today, Kat decided as she and Aidan walked to school. Even though just thinking about it made her stomach tight. What would she say? Ask her to be friends? No. Maya didn't want that. She'd made that clear. So what else?

Apologize? Tell her a joke? One or the other would be good.

I'll get it over with and do it right away, Kat thought. *I'll speak to her before school starts.*

But Grace didn't get to class until after the bell rang. Everyone was already at their desks. Grace dropped into her chair as Ms. Mitchell began the morning announcements.

Okay, I'll speak to her at morning recess, Kat said to herself. But when recess came, Ms. Mitchell asked Grace to stay inside for a chat.

Then it was lunchtime. *I'll speak to her now for sure*, thought Kat. But when the class was dismissed, Kat couldn't find Grace anywhere. Maybe she had gone home for lunch. Or maybe she was sitting alone somewhere, eating. This wasn't easy!

"Have either of you seen Grace?" she asked two girls from her class.

Lindsay and Carly just laughed. "Are you kidding?" Lindsay said. "You're not going to eat lunch with *her*, are you?"

"Good way to lose your appetite," Carly added.

Kat didn't answer.

Instead, she hurried out to find Maya. They were going to Kat's house for lunch.

But when she ran up to Maya, her friend

looked down at her feet. "I can't come to your house for lunch today," Maya said.

"Why not?" Kat was surprised. Then, worried, she asked, "Are you feeling okay?"

"Umm…" Maya glanced at Kat, and then looked away again. "No, actually, I'm not feeling great. I think it's better if I go home for lunch." She began to turn away.

"Maya, do you want me to come with you?" Kat asked.

"Uh…no. No thanks, Kat," Maya called over her shoulder, and she walked away.

Kat didn't move for a moment. Her feelings were hurt. She didn't believe Maya was feeling sick. But why wouldn't she have lunch with her? It must have something to do with Grace. Was Maya upset about Kat asking Grace to be their friend? Kat hadn't even decided if she was going to do it!

Kat could hardly eat her lunch. She was worried about Grace and Maya. Then she was angry at Grace and Maya. At the beginning of the week, she had had one best friend and no new girl in her class. Now she felt like she'd lost her best friend and the new girl hated her.

It just didn't seem fair!

Kat was a little late getting back to school after lunch, so she missed seeing Maya in the line to go inside. Was Maya really sick? Had she stayed home? Or had she come back to school? Kat didn't know. That made her angry too.

When she hurried into her own classroom, Ms. Mitchell was asking everyone to sit on the carpet at the front of the class. Kat saw

Grace sit right at the outer edge of the carpet. The other students were careful not to sit near her. It was like there was an invisible wall around Grace.

Kat was angry at her. Things had been better before she came here. But Kat also knew that she was the one who hadn't been fair. She had to do something. She got up her courage, and she sat on the edge of the carpet too. Not too close to Grace, but close enough.

"We're going to discuss temperature," Ms. Mitchell said, setting out two glasses of water.

She held up two thermometers. "Could I have two volunteers, please?"

Ms. Mitchell picked Angela and Ari. She gave them each a thermometer to put in a glass.

Then she said, "Before we look at the

thermometers, which do you think will be higher, the temperature of the cold water or the warm water?"

That was so easy. Of course the warm water would have a higher temperature than the cold water.

Kat raised her hand to answer. But Ms. Mitchell called out Grace's name, even though Grace didn't have her hand up.

"Grace," said Ms. Mitchell. "Which do you think will have the higher temperature?"

Grace flushed. She opened her mouth to answer. Then she closed it.

It was such an easy question. *Why isn't Grace answering?* Kat wondered. *Didn't she hear the question? Why doesn't she just ask Ms. Mitchell to repeat it?*

Megan snickered. She rolled her eyes, like she thought Grace was stupid.

"Grace?" Ms. Mitchell said again. "What do you think?"

But Grace said, "I don't know." She shrugged like she didn't care.

Now some of the other students giggled too. Ms. Mitchell said, "Class…" in a warning tone.

Kat frowned. Grace must be embarrassed.

But when she looked over at Grace, she couldn't believe it. Grace had that mean look on her face! She didn't look one bit embarrassed. She just looked nasty.

Kat didn't know what to think.

Then suddenly, she remembered what had happened yesterday in the park. Grace had asked if she could pet Riley. When Kat didn't answer, Grace got that mean look. Then she started to cry.

Suddenly Kat understood. The mean look meant Grace was sad and upset. It meant she was trying to stop herself from crying.

That's what she had done yesterday. And

that's what she was doing now. She just looked angry and mean, because she didn't want to cry. Maybe she was a nice person, after all. Maybe she was just unhappy about being at a new school.

Kat had planned to apologize to Grace or to tell her a joke. But now she knew she had to do more than that. Even if it made Maya upset.

CHAPTER 10

A t the end of the afternoon, Kat turned to Grace. She was about to speak, but the bell rang. Grace jumped up, grabbed her backpack, and hurried out of the classroom. She must have been waiting to make her escape.

I have to catch her! Kat thought. *I have to talk to her now!*

She ran after Grace. But, to Kat's surprise, Maya was right outside the door, waiting for her.

"Kat, I want to tell you something," Maya blurted out. She looked embarrassed. "I wasn't really sick at lunch. I was just angry. You're my best friend, and I like looking after the puppies with you. And I like doing it alone, with just you."

Kat tried to interrupt, but Maya kept going. She looked sad. "But I was thinking at lunch that you're my best friend because you're so nice. You're kind and thoughtful. And if you think Grace needs a friend—" She stopped. "I mean, if you think she needs *two* friends, then that's okay with me."

A big smile spread across Kat's face. "Maya, you're the best. I mean it!" She threw her arms around her friend and hugged her. "I *do* think Grace needs two new friends. I've got to catch up with her and tell her that," Kat said. "Even though I'm nervous!"

"Kat-Nip, I've got your back!" Maya grinned. "That's what friends are for."

The girls spotted Grace right away. She was standing near the fence. She kept glancing at the road, as if she were waiting for someone. Her face looked hard as stone.

Kat stopped in front of the new girl and took a deep breath. "Grace, can we talk to you?"

"About what?" Grace replied. She tossed her head, flipping her braids onto her back. "You didn't seem to want to talk to me in the park yesterday."

Kat turned red. "I know," she said. "I want to say I'm sorry."

Grace didn't say anything. She just pulled on the end of her braid.

Kat continued, "Grace, this my friend Maya. She's in the other fourth-grade class."

"Hi," said Maya, smiling at Grace.

Grace looked at Maya, but didn't say anything. She didn't even smile.

Kat took a deep breath and plunged ahead. "Grace, I just want to say that I know you

copied my poem, and it made me angry. But I'm sorry I didn't let you pet Riley yesterday."

"What? I didn't copy your poem," Grace blurted out. Now she looked directly at Kat. She folded her arms. "I can write my own poem. I don't need to copy yours."

Kat considered. She had seen Grace looking at her poem, but she hadn't actually seen what Grace had written. "No? Okay," she said with a shrug. "My mistake."

"And you're the one to talk anyway, sending me that rotten note." Grace glared at Kat. Her brown eyes flashed.

"Hey, I didn't write that note," Kat said, her hands on her hips. "I don't know who wrote it, but it wasn't me."

For a moment there was silence. The girls looked at each other.

"Okay. I believe you," said Grace.

Kat nodded. "And another thing. I wanted to say sorry for what I said at recess on your first day. Maya and I were talking by the big tree, and we didn't know you were there—"

"That's okay," Grace said quickly. "I didn't hear anything." But her face had turned red. She was pretending she hadn't heard.

Then Grace hoisted her backpack higher on

her back. She looked down the street again. It seemed like she was about to walk away.

"Wait, Grace," said Kat. "I want to tell you about Riley. The puppy you saw me with in the park. The one that you wanted to pet."

Grace stopped. "She's sweet," she said.

"She's so sweet," Kat agreed.

"Totally," Maya added.

Grace didn't speak for a moment. Then she said, "You're so lucky to have a dog. I used to have one. Bella. But she died a few months ago."

"Oh, that's terrible," Kat gasped.

"Mom says it's for the best. Bella was a farm dog. We had to move here, to town. Bella wouldn't have liked it," Grace said. "Mom said maybe it was better we didn't have to put her through that big change." She swallowed hard.

"Maybe," Kat agreed. "But still. You must miss her so much."

Grace nodded. "I do." Then her face went hard. Her eyes sort of bunched up.

Grace looked angry, but Kat knew she was trying not to show her real feelings.

She was trying not to cry.

"Riley isn't my puppy," Kat explained. "Or Maya's. Neither of us has our own dog. But my aunt just opened a dog-grooming salon. She's really busy, so she asked Maya and me to help out. We get to exercise any dogs she boards. This week, it's Riley. Her owners can't keep her because their daughter's allergic."

"You are so lucky," Grace said again softly.

Kat looked at Maya. Should she do it?

She didn't have to.

Just because Ms. Mitchell put Grace in the seat next to hers. Just because Grace was new and unhappy. Just because she had lost her dog. None of those things meant she had to do this.

But Maya was nodding. She even gave Kat a nudge with her elbow.

"Actually, we wanted to ask you something," Maya said.

Grace stared down at the sidewalk. Again she pulled on the end of one of her braids.

Kat started talking. "Grace, I know I haven't been very nice to you. You probably don't like me very much. I don't blame you. But would you like to come with us to play with Riley? We're on our way to see her now. It would be lots of fun."

Grace frowned. "Really? You want me to come with you?"

"Yes." Kat nodded.

"Yes," said Maya.

Grace was quiet for a moment. Slowly her frown disappeared. Her face brightened. "Well, I can't come today. My mom is picking me up and taking me to get my hair cut." She bit her lip. "But maybe I can come tomorrow. I'll ask."

"Well, I hope she says yes," said Kat. "Because, well, you know, when someone's new and you don't know her... Sometimes you may think you know right away what someone is like— just by the way she looks or acts—but actually you might be wrong."

Grace looked confused. Kat glanced at Maya

for help. "What Kat means," said Maya quickly, "is that we want to be your friends."

"Oh," Grace said. And then she smiled. Her whole face lit up.

"But, listen, there's one thing I need to warn you about, new girl," said Maya. She had on her sassy grin. Her eyes twinkled. "It's Kat. She thinks she's a comedian. She can't stop telling really terrible jokes that she thinks are hilarious."

Grace grinned. "Uh-oh," she said, going along with Maya.

"Yeah, uh-oh is right," said Maya, nodding.

"Hey, they aren't all so bad!" complained Kat, also grinning.

"Okay, Kat-Nip, prove me wrong. Tell one," challenged Maya.

"Yeah. Go for it," said Grace.

Kat thought for a minute. "How is a puppy like a penny?" she asked.

"I don't know," said Grace.

Maya shrugged. "Me neither."

"Each has a head and a tail!" Kat shouted. "Get it? A head and a tail?"

"Oh, that is such a bad joke," said Grace, but she was laughing.

"So bad." Maya was shaking her head and clutching her stomach as if she was in pain.

"I know. So bad," agreed Kat, smiling happily.

CHAPTER 11

 short time later, Kat and Maya were playing with Riley in the park.

Just like the day before, the girls stood a big distance apart and took turns calling to Riley and running with her. Riley loved the game. Her ears flew out as she bounded happily across the grass, first with one girl and then the other.

Kat tried to hold the leash out from her body when she ran. She wanted to keep Riley from coming too close to her legs. But all at once

Riley zigged and Kat zagged, and both of them fell down in a heap.

Riley took the opportunity to jump on Kat and cover her in wet dog kisses.

Click! Click!

Maya had brought her camera along. "This will be a nice photo for our Puppy Collection. We can label it *Kat and Dog!*"

"Nice one," Kat said with a grin.

"We can add it to the drawings we've made of Riley," Maya said. She snapped a few more pictures of Kat lying on her back. Kat smiled up at her and hugged Riley close.

A best friend, a new friend, and a sweet puppy to walk for a few more days! Kat thought to herself. *I am so lucky!*

 ABOUT THE AUTHOR

Award-winning author Susan Hughes has written over thirty books—both fiction and nonfiction—for children of all ages, including *Earth to Audrey, Island Horse, Four Seasons of Patrick, Off to Class: Incredible and Unusual Schools around the World,* and *Case Closed? Nine Mysteries Unlocked by Modern Science.* She is also a freelance editor and writing coach. Susan lives with her family in Toronto, Canada, in a house with a big red door—and wishes it could always be summer. You can visit her at susanhughes.ca.

Kat and Maya's
PUPPY ADVENTURES
continue with
MURPHY,
a clever sheltie
puppy!

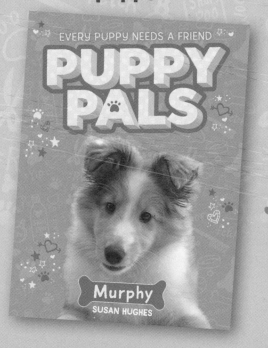

P uppies were scampering across the grass. There must have been over twenty of them! Some puppies were brown, some were black, some were brown with white spots. Some puppies had perky ears and some had floppy ears. Some had big, wide paws; some had little dainty paws. All the puppies had sparkling eyes and wagging tails.

Kat was in her classroom, sitting at her desk.

Her eyes were closed. She was having her favorite puppy daydream.

Her mother and father smile at her.

"Of course you can have a puppy, Kat," her mother says.

Her father sweeps out his arm. "Have any one you want!"

Kat smiles too. She looks at all the puppies, and she tries to choose. The little red Irish setter puppy gazing up at her with the dark-brown eyes? The black-and-white dalmatian puppy tumbling across the grass? The adorable Wheaten terrier pup with the brown face and the black muzzle?

Suddenly the bell rang. School was over for the day, and the dream ended. But that was okay. Kat had puppy plans this afternoon.

"Let's go!" Kat said to Grace, who was at the desk next to hers. The girls jumped out of their seats, grabbed their things, and made a beeline for the classroom door. But before they reached it, they heard their teacher's voice.

"Katherine, Grace, where are you off to in such a hurry?" Ms. Mitchell stood at the front of the classroom. She was smiling.

Kat liked her fourth-grade teacher a lot. For one thing, Ms. Mitchell knew how much Kat loved puppies—and her teacher liked puppies too.

"You won't believe it, Ms. Mitchell!" said Kat. "Remember how I told you my aunt opened up a dog-grooming salon? We get to help her with a puppy today!"

Ms. Mitchell smiled. "How wonderful!"

"Her business is doing really well," explained Kat. "She thought it would take some time to get going, but she was swamped with customers all last week. So she asked Maya and me to help out after school. Did you know that Grace loves puppies, just like me?"

"I had an idea that she might," Ms. Mitchell confessed, her brown eyes sparkling.

Grace chimed in, "When Kat found out, she asked me to help out at Tails Up! too!"

Grace was new to the town of Orchard Valley. She was slim with brown eyes. Grace often wore her long red hair in braids. She reminded Kat of Anne of Green Gables.

It had taken a few days, but Kat and Grace had become friends. Not best friends, like Kat and Maya—they did almost everything together. Maya liked to tease Kat and make her laugh. She said, "You love puppies, but your name is Kat? That's crazy!" In return, Kat helped Maya with school projects and told her silly jokes. They had been in the same class since kindergarten, but not this year.

But now Kat had a new friend: Grace. And Maya had agreed to try to be friends with Grace too, even though the girls didn't know each other at all, even though they didn't seem to have much in common. Grace was quiet. Maya wasn't. Grace had trouble saying how she felt about things. Maya did not.

Kat was keeping her fingers crossed that her two friends—her best friend and her new friend—would get along. This was the first time they were going to hang out together. They were going to Tails Up! together, and Kat had invited both girls to come over for dinner after. Maya had been to Kat's house at least a million times, but it would be Grace's very first time.

"Well, how lovely!" Ms. Mitchell looked pleased. "Any puppy would be very lucky to have you three looking after him. Have fun, girls!"

Kat and Grace hurried out of the school and across the playground. They stopped to look for Maya. They were all walking to Tails Up! together.

"Sorry I'm late." Maya ran up, trying to catch her breath. "Okay, let's go. But just tell me one thing: did I miss the answer to the joke?"

"Oh, right, the joke!" Grace said grinning. She rolled her eyes. Every morning, Kat told a joke. Today it was, "Why are dalmatians not good at hide-and-seek?" As usual, she made her friends wait forever before she told them the answer.

"So tell us, Kat-Nip," Maya demanded. "Answer."

"Are you sure?" Kat teased. "You don't want to guess again?"

"Oh, please. Put us out of our misery," Maya said. "Right, Grace?"

"Right!" Grace chimed in.

"Here goes: dalmatians aren't good at hide-and-seek because they're always spotted!" Kat said.

"Agh!" moaned Grace and Maya.

"Worst joke ever!" Maya complained happily, as they all rushed toward Tails Up!